Good Dog, Bonita

Friends and Amigos

titles in Large-Print Editions:

Good Dog, Bonita

BY PATRICIA REILLY GIFF

Illustrated by DyAnne DiSalvo-Ryan

Gareth Stevens Publishing
MILWAUKEE

For a free color catalog describing Gareth Stevens' list of high-quality books and multimedia programs, call 1-800-542-2595 (USA) or 1-800-461-9120 (Canada). Gareth Stevens Publishing's Fax: (414) 225-0377. See our catalog, too, on the World Wide Web: http://gsinc.com

Library of Congress Cataloging-in-Publication Data

Giff, Patricia Reilly.
  Good dog, Bonita / by Patricia Reilly Giff ; illustrated by DyAnne DiSalvo-Ryan.
    p. cm. — (Friends and amigos)
  Summary: Sarah goes to New York City with Señora Sanchez and her little dog Bonita, and when the dog runs away she feels responsible.
  ISBN 0-8368-2053-3 (lib. bdg.)
  [1. Dogs—Fiction. 2. Lost and found possessions—Fiction.
  3. New York (N.Y.)—Fiction. 4. Spanish language—Fiction.]
  I. DiSalvo-Ryan, DyAnne, ill. II. Title. III. Series: Giff, Patricia Reilly.
  Friends and amigos.
  PZ7.G3626Gm 1998
  [Fic]—dc21   97-40664

This edition first published in 1998 by
Gareth Stevens Publishing
1555 North RiverCenter Drive, Suite 201
Milwaukee, Wisconsin 53212 USA

Text © 1996 by Patricia Reilly Giff. Illustrations © 1996 by DyAnne DiSalvo-Ryan. Published by arrangement with Bantam Doubleday Dell Books for Young Readers, a division of Bantam Doubleday Dell Publishing Group, Inc., New York, New York. All rights reserved. Additional end matter © 1998 by Gareth Stevens, Inc.

Printed in the United States of America

1 2 3 4 5 6 7 8 9 02 01 00 99 98

To Christine Giff,
with love

Where to find the Spanish Lessons in this book:

Good Dog, Bonita

NEW WORDS FOR
SARAH'S SPANISH NOTEBOOK

Los números (lohs NOO-meh-rohs)	**Numbers**
1. uno (OO-noh)	one
2. dos (DOHS)	two
3. tres (TREHS)	three
4. cuatro (KWAH-troh)	four
5. cinco (SEEN-koh)	five
6. seis (SEYS)	six
7. siete (SYEH-teh)	seven
8. ocho (OH-choh)	eight
9. nueve (NWEH-veh)	nine
10. diez (DYEHS)	ten

NEW WORDS FOR
SARAH'S SPANISH NOTEBOOK

Más números (mahs NOO-meh-rohs)	More Numbers
11. once (OHN-seh)	eleven
12. doce (DOH-seh)	twelve
13. trece (TREH-seh)	thirteen
14. catorce (kah-TOHR-seh)	fourteen
15. quince (KEEN-seh)	fifteen
16. dieciséis (dyeh-see-SEYS)	sixteen
17. diecisiete (dyeh-see-SYEH-teh)	seventeen
18. dieciocho (dyeh-seeOH-choh)	eighteen
19. diecinueve (dyeh-see-NWEH-veh)	nineteen
20. veinte (VEYN-teh)	twenty

~~~~~~~~~~~~~~~~~~~~~~~~~~~~~~~~~~

1

Sarah Cole looked toward the front of the room.

The blackboard was a mess of cross-outs:

~~10 days~~

~~9 days~~

~~8 days~~

The bell rang.

Mrs. Halfpenny drew a fat yellow zero. "This is it," she said.

She began to sing. "V-a-c-a-t-i-o-n . . ."

She smiled. "Breathe in the spring air. And here's a great homework assignment. Find something new and wonderful to write about before you get back."

Sarah tried to think. What could be new and wonderful?

She watched Tuesday race to the door. "I'm off to my grandmother's for the whole week!" she was yelling.

Benjamin Bean was racing in back of her. "Me too. Me and my dog, Perro."

Sarah shoved her books into her desk.

She waited for Anna to grab her jacket.

Together they walked down the hall and out the door.

"Too bad it isn't warmer," Sarah said. "Aunt Minna could take us swimming."

Anna shook her head. "No."

"We could—" Sarah began again.

"No good," said Anna. "I'm going away." Sarah stopped walking. "¡Caramba!"

Anna put her hands up in the air. "I know. We were going to do everything. Work on Spanish . . ."

Sarah started to walk again.

Anna was always going away on vacation.

It was going to be a terrible week.

"You think I feel like going to my cousin Edna's?" Anna asked. "Pickle-face Edna?"

At the corner Anna gave her a hug. "See you in a week," she said.

Sarah nodded. She kept going . . . around the corner, up the street to her own house.

Everyone was in the kitchen.

Her mother and her little sister, Erica, were standing at the sink.

3

Their huge dog, Gus, was smushed under the table, chewing on a bagel.

And Aunt Minna, the baby-sitter, was plopping a red straw hat over her white bun.

"I'm going to Aunt Minna's house for a couple of days," Erica told Sarah.

Their mother frowned. "You're going if I ever get this gum out of your hair."

Sarah sank down in the chair. She yanked off her sneakers and put her toes on Gus's wide back.

"Erica's going away?" she asked. "Away with Aunt Minna?"

"I wanted to take both of you, but—" Aunt Minna began.

"You're going to have a bald spot the size of an egg," their mother told Erica. At the same time she winked at Aunt Minna.

"Yes, Sarah is the lucky one," said Erica.

"Shhh," said their mother. "And don't ever put a piece of gum in your mouth again."

"Especially bubble gum," said Aunt Minna. "You've got it all over the—"

"Why am I lucky?" asked Sarah.

Aunt Minna raised her eyebrows at Sarah's mother. "You'll find out."

Her mother snipped the last piece of gum out of Erica's hair. "Soon enough," she said.

NEW WORDS FOR
SARAH'S SPANISH NOTEBOOK

¿Qué hora es?	**What Time Is It?**
(KEH OH-rah EHS?)	
Es la una.	It's one o'clock.
(EHS LAH OO-nah)	
Son las dos.	It's two o'clock.
(SOHN LAHS DOHS)	
Son las tres.	It's three
(SOHN LAHS TREHS)	o'clock.
Son las cinco.	It's five o'clock.
(SOHN LAHS SEEN-koh)	
en punto	on the dot
(EHN POON-toh)	
Es mediodía.	It's noon.
(EHS meh-deeoh-DEE-ah)	
Es medianoche.	It's midnight.
(EHS meh-deeah-NOH-cheh)	
ahora	now
(ah-OH-rah)	
minuto	minute
(mee-NOO-toh)	
hora	hour
(OH-rah)	

2

Everything was quiet. Almost quiet. Gus was snoring under the table.

Aunt Minna and Erica were gone.

Her mother smiled. "Up off the chair. You'll be sleeping like Gus any minute."

"There's nothing—" Sarah began.

"Don't dare say 'nothing to do,'" her mother said. "Rush right over to Señora Sanchez's. She's waiting for you right this minute."

Sarah looked up. "Señora Sanchez?"

She was their new friend from Ecuador.

Sarah and Erica had a great time with Señora Sanchez when she baby-sat for them.

She was the world's worst housekeeper, the worst cook.

The funniest lady Sarah knew . . . and a famous artist.

Sarah reached for her jacket. She was out the door in one minute.

She counted as she raced down the street. "*Cinco . . . seis . . . siete . . . ocho . . .*

"Five . . . six . . . seven . . . eight . . ."

She banged into a tree. "*¡Caramba!*"

"Try looking where you're going," said a kid behind her.

Sarah pretended not to notice him.

She marched up the steps of the apartment house.

Señora Sanchez was at the window above her, tapping her fingers against the pane.

Her dog, Bonita, the tiniest dog in the

world, and the roundest, was standing on the windowsill.

Señora Sanchez stopped tapping. She gave Bonita a kiss and blew a bunch of kisses at Sarah.

Sarah blew a kiss back.

Inside, she didn't bother with the elevator. She took the steps two at a time. *"Dos . . . cuatro . . . seis . . . ocho."*

Señora Sanchez was waiting at the door in her fuzzy slippers.

Bonita was bouncing up and down like a tennis ball. She was white as a tennis ball, too.

Paintings were hanging all over Señora Sanchez's walls. Pictures of Ecuador with green hills and trees. Pictures of Springfield Gardens with the train at Higby Avenue, and all the kids.

Sarah breathed in.

The apartment seemed smoky. It smelled as if Señora Sanchez was cooking something. But what?

Sarah tried to hear what Señora Sanchez was saying.

Señora Sanchez lifted Bonita up. She began to dance with the dog in her arms.

Sarah smiled, watching them.

Señora Sanchez loved Bonita as much as Sarah loved Gus.

Señora Sanchez winked at her. She began to sing.

It sounded like a song Sarah's mother had been singing yesterday. Something about Spanish Harlem.

Something smelled terrible. Sarah tried to think of the word in Spanish for *kitchen,* or *stove,* or *burning.*

Instead she asked, "*¿Qué pasa?*"

Señora Sanchez stopped singing. "*¡Ca-*

ramba!" she yelled. *"Las palomitas de maíz."*

They both rushed into the kitchen.

Bonita dived in ahead of them.

Popcorn was all over the place, in bowls on the counter, on top of the stove.

Bonita bounced up and down, grabbing bites of popcorn.

"¡Mira!" said Señora. *"¡Toma!"*

Sarah took a step back. "No, *gracias,"* she said, looking at the burned popcorn.

Señora Sanchez kept speaking to her in Spanish.

Sarah didn't understand one word.

Yes. One. *Tres.* Three.

Three something.

But what?

Señora Sanchez popped a kernel of popcorn into Sarah's mouth . . . and then one into Bonita's.

"*¡Silencio!*" she told the dog.

"*¡Vete . . . rápido!*" she told Sarah. "*Adiós.*"

Before Sarah had time to say one word, Señora Sanchez had given her a little push out the door.

Bonita stood on the landing, barking, as Sarah went down the stairs again.

She stood there thinking. *Tres días.*

Three days?

Upstairs there was an explosion of sound. Sarah jumped.

Señora Sanchez had banged open the window. "Come back . . . *a mediodía,*" she called.

Mediodía. "Noon?" Sarah asked.

"*Sí. Mañana—a mediodía.*" She clicked her fingers. "*En punto.*"

Sarah nodded. She didn't know what she was nodding about, though.

"*En punto . . . en punto,*" she told herself all the way home.

By the time she reached her kitchen door, she had thought of two things.

First, *en punto* meant "on the dot."

Second, she had no idea of what was happening at noon . . . *en punto.*

NEW WORDS FOR
SARAH'S SPANISH NOTEBOOK

Expresiones (ex-preh-seeOH-nehs)	Expressions
¡Qué bueno! (KEH BWEH-noh)	Great!
¿Qué pasa? (KEH PAH-sah)	What's going on?
¡Vete! (VEH-teh)	Go away!
¡Toma! (TOH-mah)	Here you go.
¡Mira! (MEE-rah)	Look!
Un momento . . . (OONmoh-MEHN-toh)	Just a moment . . .
¡Igualmente! (ee-gwahl-MEHN-teh)	Same to you!
¡Tranquilo! (tran-KEE-loh)	Relax!
¡Fuera! (fooEH-rah)	Out!
¡Silencio! (see-LEHN-syoh)	Quiet!

3

Sarah sat in back of the taxi with Señora Sanchez and Bonita.

They were miles away from Springfield Gardens. They were in the city, in a place called Spanish Harlem.

From the window Sarah could see rows of buildings, and people sitting on the steps.

It was a good thing her mother had known what Señora Sanchez was talking about. She had helped Sarah get ready.

Sarah had been at Señora Sanchez's apartment at *mediodía en punto.*

It was the best surprise Sarah had ever had.

She'd be spending three days at Señora Sanchez's cousin's apartment. They were going to an art gallery.

They'd see Señora Sanchez's paintings . . . paintings of Ecuador, and Springfield Gardens . . .

And best of all, one of Sarah holding Bonita in her arms.

At that moment, Señora Sanchez leaned forward. "Stop, please," she told the taxi driver.

She looked at Sarah. *"Flores,"* she said. *"Para Mercedes."*

As the taxi stopped, Sarah saw a flower stand on the corner. It was filled with pink daisies and yellow daffodils. *"Un momento, por favor."* Señora Sanchez stepped out of the taxi.

At the same time, Bonita jumped out of Sarah's arms.

In two bounces, the dog was in the street.

So were a hundred cars, and taxis, and buses. And crowded on the sidewalks were soda carts, a hot dog stand, and little tables with awnings.

"*¡Caramba!*" Señora Sanchez yelled.

Sarah slid out of the car. She dropped her suitcase on the ground and dived after the dog.

She saw flashes of legs, and she could smell hot dogs, and onions, and popcorn.

Cars screeched to a stop.

Bonita didn't stop, though.

The dog was across the street in a flash.

"*Bonita,*" Señora Sanchez called.

"Come back!" Sarah shouted.

Someone else was yelling, too. "*Estúpida.*"

Sarah spun around.

It was a boy with long dark hair, and round glasses taped to his head.

"Losing the dog," he began. Then he said it again. *"Estúpida."*

He was talking to her . . . yelling at her.

And she knew what it meant.

"I am not stupid," she said.

But she didn't have time to say more than that.

Señora Sanchez was disappearing into the crowd on the other side of the street . . . and Bonita was gone.

Sarah dashed after them.

She could hear the boy following along behind her.

"Go away," she said. *"¡Vete!"*

He sped around her.

He was much faster than she was.

A moment later he caught up with Señora Sanchez.

He put his arms around her waist and spun her around.

Señora Sanchez hugged him, and kissed him, and pointed up the street to where Bonita had disappeared.

Then she pointed to Sarah.

They started to run again, past a stand with a yellow awning.

Sarah stopped for a moment, thinking.

It was no use, though.

Bonita was gone.

And suddenly Sarah realized.

So was her suitcase with her *camisas y pantalones,* her *dos dólares,* and her *cuaderno de español.*

"Estúpida," she told herself.

NEW WORDS FOR
SARAH'S SPANISH NOTEBOOK
(if she ever finds it)

• •

Julio (HOO-lyoh)	**Julio**
niño (NEE-nyoh)	boy
pelo largo (PEH-loh LAHR-goh)	long hair
corte de pelo (KOHR-teh DEH PEH-loh)	haircut
fresco (FREHS-koh)	fresh
cruel (krooEHL)	nasty
feo (FEH-oh)	ugly

4

Sarah couldn't sleep.

She could hear Señora Sanchez crying.

She was crying softly in the next bed.

Sarah knew Señora Sanchez didn't want Sarah to hear her.

Sarah had a terrible lump in her throat.

She knew Señora Sanchez was thinking about Bonita.

Poor Bonita.

Where was she now?

Sarah turned over.

And where was her suitcase?

Right now she was wearing Julio's pajamas.

HOO-lyoh's pajamas.

Fat green ones with alligators or crocodiles crawling all over them.

Terrible.

Estúpido.

She thought back to this afternoon.

She and Señora Sanchez and Julio had combed the streets.

Up one street, cross over, down the next, calling for Bonita.

They had passed little grocery stores with piles of fruit and flowers. The signs read: FRUTAS Y FLORES. Bodegas, they were called.

They had wandered into restaurants with wonderful smells. Chicken and rice, Sarah thought.

Arroz con pollo.

They had been too worried to eat, though.

They had only told everyone to be on the lookout for a little dog that bounced around like a tennis ball.

At least that was what Sarah thought Julio was saying in Spanish.

He didn't bother to ask anyone about her suitcase.

They had stopped on one corner where boys were playing music.

They were playing on huge tin cans and drums.

The sound made Sarah tap her feet and want to dance.

"Hola," the boys had said, and they had shaken their heads. "No."

They hadn't seen a little dog, either.

At last Julio had brought them to this apartment.

Julio, Señora Sanchez's cousin's son.

Julio with ears as big as an elephant's.

Julio who needed a *corte de pelo*.

Julio was very *fresco*.

Señora Sanchez's cousin was waiting for them with hugs and kisses and *arroz con jamón y ensalada y torta*. Rice and ham, salad and cake.

But still no one could eat.

Even the cousin, Mercedes, had tears in her eyes when she heard that Bonita, the smallest dog in the world, was wandering somewhere in the middle of the city.

The poor dog would have nothing to eat . . . nowhere to sleep.

Sarah turned over again.

She tried not to think about the cars

whizzing by . . . cars that would never see a tiny little dog.

Sarah wished she were home.

She wished she had never come.

And what about her suitcase?

And being stuck here for three days with Julio, who wouldn't speak English to her . . . Julio, who thought she was *estúpida.*

NEW WORDS FOR
SARAH'S SPANISH NOTEBOOK

• •

PLACES TO LOOK FOR BONITA
(AND THE SUITCASE)

La ciudad *(LAH seeoo-DAHD)*	**The City**
casa refugio para animales *(KAH-sah reh-FOO-hyoh* *PAH-rah ah-nee-MAH-lehs)*	animal shelter
apartamentos *(ah-pahr-tah-MEHN-tohs)*	apartments
tienda *(teeEHN-dah)*	store
supermercado *(soo-pehr-mehr-KAH-doh)*	supermarket

NEW WORDS FOR
SARAH'S SPANISH NOTEBOOK

PLACES TO LOOK FOR BONITA
(AND THE SUITCASE)

restaurante   restaurant
(rehs-taaoo-RAHN-teh)

parque   park
(PAHR-keh)

escuela   school
(ehs-KWEH-lah)

metro   subway
(MEH-troh)

¿Dónde está Bonita?   Where is
*(DOHN-deh ehs-TAH   Bonita?
boh-NEE-tah)*

¿Dónde está la maleta?   Where is the
*(DOHN-deh ehs-TAH   suitcase?
LAH mah-LEH-tah)*

5

And then at last it was morning.

Sarah looked out the window at the bright sun and the roofs of the apartment houses.

Everything sparkled. It was going to be a beautiful day . . . except that she had to wear the same clothes she had worn yesterday.

The shirt had *arroz con jamón* stains.

And she had spilled milk in a line down her jeans.

She threw on her clothes anyway and

went into the kitchen. It was all her fault that Bonita had jumped out of the car.

Her fault, the whole thing.

And it seemed that Julio was saying that right now. He tossed his head at her and muttered something she couldn't understand.

Then he took a mouthful of cereal, a huge mouthful.

Sarah's mother would have had a fit if she and Erica had eaten like that.

"*Péinate el pelo,*" he told her.

Pelo. Hair. What was he talking about? Her hair? She smoothed it down.

"*Gorila,*" he said, and laughed.

She opened her mouth. Was he calling her a gorilla?

"*Igualmente,*" she said without thinking. It was a word she and Anna had used on Benjamin in their class.

The same to you.

She swallowed. If only she were home, home at her house with her mother and father, and Gus.

Señora Sanchez and Mercedes came into the kitchen. *"Ah, café,"* said Mercedes.

Señora Sanchez smiled at Sarah. She poured her a large glass of orange juice.

"Toma, querida," said Señora Sanchez.

Querida, darling. It was what Señora Sanchez always called her . . . or *angelita.*

This morning Señora Sanchez's eyes were red and a little puffy. She looked sad even when she was smiling at Sarah.

"Today the art gallery," Señora Sanchez said. "And signs for Bonita." She hammered up invisible signs. "On the telephone poles . . ."

"You'll find Bonita," said Mercedes. *"Tranquila."*

34

Julio pulled paper out of a drawer. He began to write:

PERRO PERDIDO
por ~~absurda~~ niña estúpida
REWARD
Maleta perdida también

Sarah leaned across the table. She tried to read what he had written.

Perro was dog, she knew that. *Perdido* must mean lost.

Señora Sanchez was leaning over the table, too. She was pointing at the second line:

por ~~absurda~~ niña estúpida

She shook her head. *"No, Julio."*

Julio laughed. He began to erase.

But not before Sarah had figured out what it said. *Por ~~absurda~~ niña estúpida.* By a stupid ~~silly~~ girl.

That Julio.

Sarah looked at the last line. Simple. *Suitcase lost too.*

Then everything was rushed. Señora Sanchez was looking for her purse. Mercedes was cleaning the breakfast table. And Julio . . .

Who knew what Julio was doing?

They were out the door and down the street, almost running, a few minutes later. First they left Julio's sign at Paul's Print Shop to be copied. Then they took a bus to the art gallery.

The gallery was white: walls, floor, and ceiling. It was bright and clean, and a man was beginning to hang Señora Sanchez's paintings.

A woman came forward. She was smiling at Señora Sanchez, bowing a little. She spoke first in Spanish, then in English.

She told them the rest of the paintings

would be hanging soon. *A mediodía en punto.* At noon on the dot.

Sarah had to smile a little, even though she felt terrible: sad, and messy. Even though she knew she had spoiled this special day for Señora Sanchez.

In a half hour, Julio's signs—hot pink— were ready. The three of them left these everywhere they could, on telephone poles, in store windows, and even propped up on benches.

And everywhere they went, they asked about Bonita.

No one had seen a tiny white dog with pointy ears.

NEW WORDS FOR
SARAH'S SPANISH NOTEBOOK

| **Tú y yo** | **You and Me** |
| *(TOO EE YOH)* | |

| yo | I |
| *(YOH)* | |

| tú | you |
| *(TOO)* | |

| usted | you |
| *(oohs-TEHD)* | |

| él | he |
| *(EHL)* | |

| ella | she |
| *(EH-yah)* | |

| nosotros | we |
| *(noh-SOH-trohs)* | |

| nosotras | we (all girls) |
| *(noh-SOH-trahs)* | |

| ellos | they |
| *(EH-yohs)* | |

| ellas | they (all girls) |
| *(EH-yahs)* | |

Sarah stood on the corner with Señora Sanchez and Julio.

Suddenly she had an idea.

The animal shelter.

Maybe someone had dropped Bonita off there.

Maybe she was sitting in a cage, just waiting for them.

She tried to think of the word for *animal*. It was almost the same.

El animal . . . ah-nee-MAHL.

Easiest thing in the world.

But shelter?

"*El animal,*" she began aloud, and stopped.

"Say it in English," Julio said.

"An animal shelter," she began again.

"*Muy bien,*" he said, sounding surprised.

He spoke to Señora Sanchez in Spanish. The words were fast, so fast that Sarah could understand only two or three.

A moment later Señora Sanchez was hugging her. "Yes," she said. "*Sí.*"

They followed Julio into the subway. They rode two stops to a long, low brick building.

Inside were pictures of dogs, and cats, and birds, and even a small gray mouse.

A woman with a braid hanging over one shoulder smiled at them. "Looking for a new pet?" she asked. "I have the perfect—"

"Dog," said Julio.

"Cat," said the woman.

"Tiny dog," said Sarah.

"Big cat," said the woman.

"*Bonita,*" said Señora Sanchez.

"Toughy," said the woman.

They stood there for a second, shaking their heads.

Then the woman sighed.

"You've lost your dog. Let's take a look," she said.

In the back were cages. There were tiny dogs, and white dogs, and . . .

"Look at this cat," Julio said.

The cat was big and orange. He had a million scars.

"Great cat," said Julio, and he put his fingers through the holes in the cage.

The cat stared at him. Then he rubbed his large orange head against Julio's fingers.

"I told you," said the woman. "That's Toughy."

"But . . . ," Senora Sanchez began.

"I know," said the woman sadly. "It's not your dog. But this cat needs a home so much."

They all shook their heads one last time, listening to the cat crying after them.

He cried after them as they left.

Sarah felt like putting her hands over her ears. She felt like running back to take the cat.

Julio was standing at the door. She couldn't believe it. He looked as if he wanted to cry.

The lady with the braid looked at them.

"It's hard to find a home for such a big cat."

Sarah looked at Julio.

He stared back. Then he marched out the door without another word.

NEW WORDS FOR
SARAH'S SPANISH NOTEBOOK

Buscar	**To Look For**
(boohs-KAHR)	
Yo busco . . .	I look for . . .
(YOH BOOHS-koh)	
Tú buscas . . .	You look for . . .
(TOO BOOHS-kahs)	
Usted busca . . .	You look for . . .
(oohs-TEHD BOOHS-kah)	
Julio busca al gato.	Julio looks for the cat.
(HOO-lyoh BOOHS-kah AHL GAH-toh)	
Sarah busca la maleta.	Sarah looks for the suitcase.
(SAH-rah BOOHS-kah LAH mah-LEH-tah)	
Todo el mundo busca a Bonita.	Everybody is looking for Bonita.
(TOH-doh EHL MOON-doh BOOHS-kah AH boh-NEE-tah)	

7

"¿*Mediodía en punto?*" Señora Sanchez asked.

"That means 'noon on the dot,'" Julio told Sarah.

"I know that," Sarah said quickly. She said it nicely, though.

Julio looked almost as sad as Señora Sanchez. His large ears were red, and so was his face.

Julio looked at the little round watch on his wrist. He drew in his breath.

47

Señora Sanchez looked at her watch, too. "*¡Caramba!*" she yelled. "*¡Es la una!*"

They were an hour late.

They stood there for one more second; then they raced for the subway.

It seemed to take forever to get to the gallery. The train didn't come for several minutes, and then it was slow.

When they finally opened the door to the large white gallery room, people were there already.

Cousin Mercedes rushed over with the gallery woman. They were both talking in Spanish.

Sarah understood only a few words. Enough to know that everyone had been worried about them.

"Bonita?" Mercedes asked.

Sarah turned away.

She didn't want to hear what Señora Sanchez would say. She didn't want to see her sad face.

Then she drew in her breath.

The room was beautiful.

Yellow flowers filled vases in the corners. Pots of ivy trailed from the windowsills.

Best of all were Señora Sanchez's paintings.

In the clear white light, the colors seemed even more beautiful than they had in Señora Sanchez's living room.

Sarah wandered around looking at the green hills of Ecuador . . . the red railroad station that looked just like the one at Higby Avenue.

She hardly paid attention to the woman who handed her a small glass of soda.

She stopped in the center of the room.

There, on an easel, was her picture. Hers and Bonita's.

She was wearing a white shirt, and she was smiling.

It seemed as if Bonita were smiling, too.

Her little ears were straight up, and her eyes were dark and shiny.

Sarah stood there for a long time.

She liked the way she looked. She liked the tiny locket Señora Sanchez had painted on the shirt.

Other people walked by.

"Wonderful," they were saying. *"¡Qué bueno!"*

Sarah watched while a Spanish-speaking woman with large eyeglasses stopped in front of her painting.

The woman leaned closer.

Then she turned to the man who was standing next to her.

"¡Mira!" she said. *"¡Es el perro perdido!"*

NEW WORDS FOR
SARAH'S SPANISH NOTEBOOK

Encontrar (ehn-kohn-TRAHR)	**To Find**
Yo encuentro (YOH ehn-KWEHN-troh)	I find
Tú encuentras (TOO ehn-KWEHN-trahs)	You find
Usted encuentra (oohs-TEHD ehn-KWEHN- trah)	You find
Sarah encuentra a Julio. (SAH-rah ehn-KWEHN-trah AH HOO-lyoh)	Sarah finds Julio.
Julio encuentra al gato. (HOO-lyoh ehn-KWEHN-trah AHL GAH-toh)	Julio finds the cat.
La señora Sanchez encuentra a Bonita. (LAH seh-NYOH-rah SAHN-chehs ehn-KWEHN-trah AH boh-NEE-tah)	Mrs. Sanchez finds Bonita.

Señora Sanchez was laughing. She was crying.

Everyone else had tears in their eyes, too.

It had taken the woman five minutes to explain. First in Spanish. Then to Sarah in English.

"Palomitas de maíz," she kept saying as she shook her head.

She owned a small cart with a yellow awning, and she sold popcorn. "The little dog loves *palomitas de maíz*," she said.

It took the woman another twenty minutes to jump into a cab and bring Bonita to the gallery.

The little dog leaped out of her arms and raced for Señora Sanchez. In one bounce she was in her arms.

Everyone was clapping.

Then they all turned to look at the painting.

All except for the woman, who was handing Sarah her suitcase. "Right in the middle of the street," she told Sarah. "I knew it had to belong with the little dog."

Julio wasn't looking at the painting, either.

"*Vámonos,*" he was telling Sarah. "Come on. *Son las cinco.*"

"Where are you going?" Sarah asked.

Julio raised his shoulders high in the air and dropped them. "Where do you think?"

Sarah looked back at her suitcase against

the wall. Wherever they were going, she should change her clothes.

Julio was yanking her by the arm. He looked at his watch.

Sarah looked back once more.

Señora Sanchez was talking to a group of people. She waved one arm at a painting and held Bonita in the other.

She blew Sarah a kiss. *"Hasta luego,"* she called.

Then Sarah was out the door, following Mercedes and Julio down the subway steps.

"¿Qué pasa?" Sarah asked Mercedes.

Mercedes turned to Julio. She rolled her eyes. *"Un gato, no,"* she said. "I don't want a cat . . ."

"*Sí,* you're going to love this cat," Julio said. "He's big, he's orange, he's tough."

"¿Gato?" Sarah asked. "The cat at the animal shelter?"

"He needs a home," Julio said. "A place where he's safe . . . a place where he won't get into fights."

Mercedes sighed. "Do I need a cat?" she asked Sarah.

"Wait and see," Julio said. "You're going to love him."

He stood up as the train reached the station. "Hurry. The shelter closes in three minutes."

They rushed down the street and around the corner.

Too late.

Church bells rang five times.

The shelter door was locked.

Julio's mouth turned down.

Poor Julio, Sarah thought.

Then she saw movement behind the window.

"Wait," she said.

The woman with the braid unlocked the door. *"Tranquilo,"* she said. "I've been waiting for you. I knew you'd be back. The cat is waiting for you, too."

NEW WORDS FOR
SARAH'S SPANISH NOTEBOOK

MERCEDES'S TROPICAL FRUIT MILK SHAKE
(to make in a blender)

Receta para un batido *(reh-SEH-tah PAH-rah* *OON bah-TEE-doh)*	**Recipe for a Milk Shake**
ingredientes *(een-greh-deeEHN-tehs)*	ingredients
una taza de leche *(OOH-nah TAH-sah* *DEH LEH-cheh)*	one cup of milk
dos cucharaditas de azúcar *(DOHS koo-chah-rah-DEE-* *tahs DEH ah-SOO-kahr)*	two teaspoons of sugar

NEW WORDS FOR
SARAH'S SPANISH NOTEBOOK

· ·

MERCEDES'S TROPICAL FRUIT MILK SHAKE

dos cubitos de hielo *(DOHS koo-BEE-tohs deh YEH-loh)*	two cubes of ice
una fruta *OO-nah FROO-tah*	one piece of fruit
banana *(bah-NAH-nah)*	banana
mango *(MAHN-goh)*	mango
papaya *(pah-PAH-yah)*	papaya
coco *(KOH-koh)*	coconut

Someone had pushed back the couch in Mercedes's living room.

People were crowded around Señora Sanchez, smiling and talking.

Mercedes was bringing in trays of food to put on the end tables.

Someone had put music on, and a couple of people were beginning to dance.

Sarah took two tiny meatballs and dropped one on the floor for Bonita.

Then she went to see where Julio was.

She found him in the kitchen, watching the cat.

Toughy was marching across the table, tail up, and Julio was laughing.

He stopped short as Mercedes came back into the kitchen.

Even the cat knew enough to dive off the table.

Mercedes was scolding in Spanish. She spoke so quickly that Sarah could catch only three words: *gato, mesa,* and *¡fuera!*

Cat, table, and out the door.

It was enough for Sarah to understand.

She knew Mercedes didn't mean it, though.

Julio knew, too.

He was grinning at Sarah, and she was grinning back.

She couldn't believe it.

Julio was her *amigo*.

He wasn't *feo* anymore. He wasn't *fresco*.

He leaned forward. "You look better," he said.

She could feel Toughy winding himself around her legs.

"What do you mean 'better'?" she asked.

"Not *fea*." He shoved a potato chip into his mouth. "Not a *gorila*."

She took a breath. That Julio.

Then she laughed.

She could feel Toughy trying to climb her leg. He dug sharp claws into her ankle.

Gently she pried him off her leg and sank down on the floor to pet him.

Then she thought of Mrs. Halfpenny, and going back to school on Monday.

She thought about her homework. She

had to write about something new and wonderful that had happened.

Tomorrow Señora Sanchez had promised to take them to a movie in Spanish.

And Mercedes was going to teach her how to make a *batido de frutas*—a tropical fruit milk shake.

She looked out the window. She could see the lights of Spanish Harlem.

It would take forever for her to write about all the new and wonderful things she had seen.

But right now, Señora Sanchez had come into the kitchen. She gave Sarah and Julio a hug and pulled them toward the living room.

A line of people was dancing around the living room and down the hall.

"*¡Bailan!*" Señora Sanchez said.

Sarah didn't know how.

Julio probably didn't, either.

She was going to try, though.

It was one more new and wonderful thing.

LETTER TO LIBRARIANS, TEACHERS, AND PARENTS

Learning a new language can be intimidating. *Friends and Amigos* introduces a basic Spanish vocabulary in a challenging, yet familiar setting. New words are interspersed throughout each chapter and can be assimilated easily and naturally as young readers enjoy the story. The reinforcement that is so important in developing language skills is encouraged at the end of each chapter, where a list of words introduced in the previous pages offers pronunciation guides and basic definitions. *Friends and Amigos* also offers real-life stories that center around bilingual friendships, thus encouraging readers to recognize the tremendous value of cultural diversity in the world community.

The intriguing activities on page 68 help learning take place while having fun. Parents and teachers can incorporate many of these activities on a daily basis. The recommended books, videos, and web sites that follow on page 69 also help provide an enjoyable pathway to learning more about Spanish language and culture. These positive experiences will encourage young readers to explore a language other than their own.

ACTIVITIES

. . . .

Play bingo. Using an ordinary bingo game, play bingo with friends. Gather inexpensive prizes, such as wrapped candy, simple toys, crayons, or used paperback books. Take turns being the caller. Call out the letters and numbers in Spanish. The first to have "bingo" must read back the winning letters and numbers in Spanish. The winners can choose their prize if they can name it in Spanish; for example, *dulce* for "candy."

City sight-seeing. Choose a large city in a Spanish-speaking country. Plan a visit to that city for three or four days. Travel guides from the library will help you choose interesting sights to see. Make out a schedule of sight-seeing and other activities for each day. Select a good place to stay overnight. Be sure to include restaurants for each meal.

Imaginary zoo. Cut out pictures or make drawings of animals you might find in a zoo. On large sheets of white paper, outline enclosures for each animal and use crayons, watercolors, or color pencils to draw in the proper environment for that animal, such as desert, grassland, ice floe, or any other. Glue the animal pictures in their habitats. Make labels in Spanish for each animal, its environment, where it is from, and what it eats.

MORE BOOKS TO READ

Children of Ecuador. Connie Bickman (Abdo & Daughters)

Chile. Karen Jacobsen (Childrens Press)

El Salvador in Pictures. Nathan Haverstock (Lerner)

Mexico. Festivals of the World series. Elizabeth Berg (Gareth Stevens)

Peru. Festivals of the World series. Leslie Jermyn (Gareth Stevens)

Puerto Rico. Festivals of the World series. Erin Foley (Gareth Stevens)

Spanish for Children: For Young Learners. Catherine Bruzzone (NTC Publishing Group)

VIDEOS

Ecuador. (AGC Educational Media)

Good Trip, Señorita Fernandez. (Agency for Instructional Technology)

Life in Small Hispanic Towns. (Video Knowledge)

Where Animals Live. (GPN)

WEB SITES

www.nationalgeographic.com/resources/ngo/maps/atlas/samerica.html

www.nationalgeographic.com/resources/ngo/maps/atlas/namerica/namerica.html

69

Patricia Reilly Giff is the author of many fine books for children, including *The Kids of the Polk Street School* (series), *The Lincoln Lions Band* (series), *The Polka Dot Private Eye* (series), and *New Kids at the Polk Street School* (series). Ms. Giff received her bachelor's degree from Marymount College and a master's degree in history from St. John's University. She holds a Professional Diploma in Reading and a Doctorate of Humane Letters from Hofstra University. She was a teacher and reading consultant for many years. Ms. Giff lives in Weston, Connecticut.

DyAnne DiSalvo-Ryan has illustrated numerous books for children, including some she has written herself. She lives in Haddonfield, New Jersey.